THE DAY THE GYPSIES CAME TO TOWN

Story by
Audrey Nelson Masterson

Illustrations by
Douglas Oudekerk

A Carnival Press Book Raintree Publishers Inc.

"Wake up, Abby!" said Uncle Will as he brought up a pail of fresh milk. "I've got news."

Abby slumped in the porch swing. "What news?" she groaned. "Nothing ever happens in Renville."

Uncle Will tugged on her hair ribbon. "You're wrong about that, little lady," he teased. "Today the Gypsies are coming to town!"

"Gypsies? Who are the Gypsies? Where do they come from?"

"I'm not sure," said Uncle Will. "Gypsies are wanderers. They travel all over the world. And today they're coming to Renville."

Abby's mother stepped outside to get the milk. "Did you say Gypsies? In Renville?"

"That's right," replied Uncle Will. "Folks say they have healing powers and secret potions."

"Secret potions?" Abby jumped up from the swing. "Really, Uncle Will?"

"I've heard they can talk to animals and tell fortunes, too. Keep a lookout, Abby. Maybe they'll come this way."

Abby grabbed her spyglass and ran down the steps. "Now, Abby," called her mother, "I don't want you running off looking for Gypsies. Stay in the park. If you see any strangers, keep to yourself. And no spying!"

Abby ran to the park and ducked into a thick bower of lilac bushes. This was her Hiding House. She bent back a branch and watched for the Gypsies. None came — only Jimmy Kramer and his whiney little brother, and Mrs. Harvey's freckled cat.

Clang! Clink! Clang! Abby jumped. *Could this be the Gypsies?* But it was only Hank, the ice man, heavy ice-tongs banging against the side of his cart.

Then Abby saw Mr. Hawkins' water wagon, sprinkling the dusty road. "I see the water wagon every day," she complained. She pulled out her spyglass for a closer look, but the street was empty.

"Never mind," she sighed. "I'll look for four-leaf clovers instead."

But before long, she heard creaking noises. Dogs barked and horses whinnied. Abby scrambled to her knees and spread the branches.

Just then, a line of brightly painted wagons turned the corner. These were no ice carts! These were real Gypsy caravans with fancy woodwork and colorful trim.

"So many horses!" murmured Abby. In her spyglass, they seemed close enough to touch — husky draft horses, small spotted ponies and a pair of beautiful Arabian horses with braided tails.

Suddenly, Abby saw the lead wagon veer off the road and pull into the park. Soon, the other wagons followed, forming a circle around Abby's Hiding House. "They're all around me!" she gasped.

Abby pulled her knees to her chin and stayed very still as the Gypsies made camp. The lead driver unharnessed his horse and tied it to a lilac branch. Abby held her breath as the horse nibbled the leaves near her foot.

Suddenly, the branches parted. A young Gypsy poked his head inside. "I caught you!" he bragged. "A *rakli!* Do you know what we do with *raklies* who sneak into our camp?"

"But I didn't sneak in," cried Abby. "This is my Hiding House. I was here first."

"You're right," said the boy. "I snuck in. I am Jasper, the master sneak. Watch!" Jasper picked up Abby's three biggest marbles and juggled them back and forth until one disappeared.

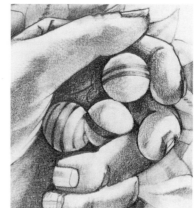

rakli — a non-Gypsy girl

Before Abby could stop him, Jasper grabbed her chalk slate. "Aha!" he exclaimed, "you can write. Write my name."

Abby's fingers trembled as she picked up the chalk. She wasn't sure how to spell "Jasper," but she did her best.

Jasper grinned as he traced the letters of his name. "And what are you called?" he asked.

"My name is Abby."

"Too dull," said Jasper. "I will call you Serena...Princess Serena. And this will be the dungeon where you live."

"No!" cried Abby. "I live in the brown house across the street, but I can't get home."

"You see?" said Jasper. "You're trapped. And only I can help you escape."

"Would you?" Abby pleaded. "Please."

"What will you give me if I do?" Jasper demanded. Abby didn't know what to say. She pointed to the chalk slate on Jasper's lap. "*Boktalo*," he whispered. "It's a deal."

Boktalo — Lucky me

Jasper snatched the spyglass and scanned the camp. "Do you see the *vardo* with the painted wheels?" Abby nodded. "Let's make a run for it. Ready? Go!"

Together, they dashed across the clearing and slid under the nearest wagon. Abby crouched behind a kettle and tried to catch her breath. From there, she could see the whole Gypsy camp.

Children laughed as they ran into the creek to bathe. The older boys fetched water while the girls gathered wood. Dogs spread out, sniffing for game, and chickens ran loose around the campfires where the women made stew.

"Who is that man with the bird squawking on his hat?" Abby whispered.

Jasper spoke softly. "That is Old Anselo, our leader, and his pet. Old Anselo is tending the sick colt, but the myna bird is scolding him, demanding food."

Jasper waited until the younger men headed toward town to sell horses. Then, when no one was looking, he pointed to a ladder and followed Abby into his family's wagon.

Vardo — Gypsy house wagon

Inside, Jasper's sister Morjiana sat braiding her hair. Seeing Abby, she stood up and backed away.

"It's alright," Jasper told her. "Abby's a friend." Morjiana frowned. She didn't trust strangers.

"Please," said Abby, "don't tell them I'm here." She pulled a ribbon from her hair and offered it to Morjiana. Morjiana stared at Abby's short calico dress and brand new sandals. Silently, she took the ribbon, pinned up her braids and tied an apron over her skirts.

Abby had never seen such an apron — swirling with embroidered flowers and birds. *And the jewelry!* Bangles jingled on Morjiana's wrists. Loops of gold flashed in her ears as she stepped from the wagon.

"Quick, Abby, close the window sashes while I keep watch," Jasper told her.

Abby climbed onto a high bed and closed the curtains on the back window. "Is this where you sleep?" she said. "It's like a cupboard bed."

"If it's warm, we sleep outside around the fire," said Jasper. "Father tells stories and Mother sings. We fall asleep watching the stars."

Abby peeked out the window. "Where are all the women going?" she asked.

"They're going out selling and *dukkering*," said Jasper. "Now's our chance to get away."

But as soon as Jasper opened the wagon doors, a lurcher dog came bounding across camp, barking loudly. As it neared the wagon, it stiffened and growled at Abby. Hearing the commotion, the children came running.

Frightened, Abby leapt from the ladder and bolted across camp, scattering a sheaf of straw and trampling herbs that lay drying in the sun. Just as she reached her front stoop, she heard Jasper behind her.

"What are you doing here?" asked Abby, gulping for air.

"You saw my home," said Jasper. "Now, I will see yours."

"Shh...." said Abby. "My mother is out back in the garden. We'll have to be very quiet."

"I'm thirsty," said Jasper as they tiptoed into the kitchen. "Where is your water pump?"

"We use a sink instead," said Abby, turning on the faucet. Sploosh! The water gushed out.

"Magic!" cried Jasper. "How did you do it?" Jasper played with the faucet until his shirt was wet from splashing. "What's this?" he asked, pointing to a tall metal box.

"That's the ice-box," said Abby. "Look inside."

Jasper's eyes grew wide. He had seen icicles before, but never a huge block of ice like this. "*Dilo!*" he muttered. "Ice in a box!"

"I have something even better," Abby told him. She took out a canning jar and poured a bubbly brown liquid into two tall glasses. "It's root beer," she said. "I made it myself."

Jasper sniffed at the frothy drink, then gulped it down and poured some more. "*Dordi! Dordi!*" he cried. "It fizzles."

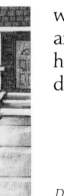

Just then, the doorbell rang. "Hurry," Abby whispered, "into the pantry. Mother is coming to answer the door." Abby shut the pantry door just as her mother came in. When Abby heard the front door open, she shooed Jasper out the back.

Dilo! — Silly, crazy!
Dordi! Dordi! — Well! Well!

"Abby, come back tonight," said Jasper. "Mother will sing and Father will play his violin. We could watch the dancing from your Hiding House."

"I can't," said Abby. "I might get caught."

"You won't get caught," Jasper insisted. "I have a plan. As soon as it gets dark, meet me at the footbridge outside our camp." Jasper ran off before Abby could say no.

On the front porch, three Gypsy women were selling handmade articles. "Clothespins! Baskets! Good luck charms!" they called out. "Sharpen your knives? Tell your fortune?" Abby's mother bought a dozen clothespins.

"Ah!" sighed the fortuneteller, as Abby stepped outside, "I see your daughter wants to hear her fortune." The old woman reached for Abby's hand and studied the lines in her palm. "Mmm...you've got no common hand, child. I see changes coming soon...an adventure you will remember all your life long. And here, I see signs of fame. Yes, yes, you will be a famous singer or dancer, perhaps."

"Did you hear that, Mother? I'm going to be famous," Abby shouted.

"It's only a fortune," said her mother. "Now go in and start the potatoes for supper."

Abby was so excited she peeled fifteen potatoes. All during supper she thought about the Gypsy fortuneteller and Jasper's plan. She ate quickly and asked to be excused.

As Abby crossed the park, she saw the Gypsy campfire blazing in the distance. She leaned against the footbridge and waited. The night was filled with the smell of burning wood and spicy stew.

"*Alloo*, Abby! It's me," called Jasper as he climbed out from under the bridge. "Look what I brought for you." He handed Abby a bundle of skirts and petticoats. "Put them on and you won't have to hide," he said.

"Gypsy clothes," cried Abby. "But how did you get them?"

"I *found* them," said Jasper, emptying jewelry from his pockets. "Tomorrow, they must be back where I found them. Tonight, they are yours."

Abby's heart pounded with excitement as she put on the Gypsy jewelry and clothes. She pinned up her braids like Morjiana's, kicked off her shoes and twirled around on the bridge. "I feel like Princess Serena," she said. "No one will ever know it's me."

"Not if you have a charm," said Jasper. He handed Abby a small wooden colt, carved out of pine. "Put this in your pocket for luck," he told her. "I whittled it with my own knife."

Alloo! — Hello!

The sweet, clear whine of violins echoed through the park. Abby and Jasper ran toward the campfire and slipped into the crowd of Gypsies.

Abby watched Old Anselo clapping — slowly at first, then faster and faster until everyone was clapping, even the children.

Then, the beat changed. The violins rushed into a new song and the Gypsies started dancing. "Follow me," Jasper hollered, and he pulled Abby into the circle.

When Jasper clapped, Abby clapped. When Jasper stomped and shouted, Abby stomped and shouted outloud. Together, they clicked their tongues and scuffed their heels as the circle moved round and round.

Before long, the Gypsies were singing. Their bold voices drowned out the music. Abby kicked and whirled until the whole camp was a blur of laughter and song.

"Sing!" shouted Jasper. "Sing along!"

So Abby sang, louder than she had ever sung before. The words felt strange and mysterious on her lips, but in her heart Abby felt like a real Gypsy.

Then, suddenly, Abby heard the ringing of the nine o'clock bell. "I've got to go," she cried. "I'm supposed to be home by now." She broke away from the circle and ran.

"Wait!" called Jasper. "You can't go home dressed like that."

"I almost forgot," said Abby. She slipped out of the Gypsy clothes and reached into her pocket. "This is for you, Jasper, so you can learn to write your name." Abby held out her box of chalk.

Again, the nine o'clock bell rang. Abby pulled the bangles from her wrists and took the charm from her pocket.

"Keep it," said Jasper, as he pressed the colt into Abby's hand. "It will bring you good luck. *Kushti bok,* Abby!"

Jasper watched as Abby ran up the street to her house. He saw her look back, just as she reached the porch. A moment later, the front door closed.

"*Kushti bok,*" Abby whispered, as she turned off the light.

Kushti bok — Good luck

Notes about Jasper's people:

rom

The Gypsy word for *man* or *husband* is *rom*.

Rom

Rom, with a capital "R," is the name of the traveling Gypsies, also called *Romanies.*

Almost a thousand years ago, the Romany people left India and began to travel north and west through Europe, Asia and the Middle East. When they split up and traveled to different countries, separate tribes were formed.

Anglo-Rom

Jasper's tribe were *Anglo-Rom,* or English Gypsies. In the late seventeenth century, the English government sent Gypsies to colonize the New World. Many Gypsies came to America as indentured servants or outcasts. Jasper's story takes place in 1925.

Romnichels

Jasper's people called themselves *Romnichels* (the Gypsy fellows). The Romnichels bred and trained horses and hunting dogs, which they sold at fairs through the United States. Some Romnichels were famous boxers. Others collected and sold scrap metal for a living.

In the warm seasons, when they traveled, the women sold handmade clothespins, brooms, paper flowers and lace, and also told fortunes.

Vardos

In the winter, the Romnichels traveled south to camp. They kept their wagons warm with cast iron stoves, and lit their wagons with kerosene lamps.

The Gypsies were strict about keeping their homes clean. The fancier *vardos* (house wagons) had brilliant-cut mirrors, ornamental brasswork, painted scrollwork and lace trimmings. Gypsies often hung horseshoes in their homes to ward off evil spirits.

Today, there may be as many as 750,000 Rom Gypsies in the United States.

Drom

Drom is the Romany word for *road*. The road is the real home of the Rom, for they have been traveling and setting up camp (*hatchintan*) for nearly a thousand years.

Why did the Gypsies leave India? No one knows.

Why do they travel? Some Gypsies say they are the grasshoppers in a world of ants.

Romanes

How do we know the Gypsies came from India?

Sanskrit is an ancient language of India. The Romany language, called *Romanes*, is similar to Sanskrit. For example, the Romany word *pal* comes from the Sanskrit word for *brother*.

In English, we call a friend a *pal*, but *pal* is not an English word. It is a word we borrowed from the Gypsies.

Because Romanes is not a written language, Jasper did not learn to write. Instead, he learned about his people by listening to his grandmother tell stories about Gypsy ancestors and beliefs.

Gypsies told stories so well, and listened so carefully, they didn't need history books or storybooks. They used memory and imagination instead.

Audrey Nelson Masterson has worked with children all her life as a teacher, mother, and grandmother. Active in the daycare movement, her varied interests also include art, theatre, dance, and music. A graduate of the University of Minnesota, she lives in Minneapolis with her husband, an inventor and consulting engineer. An accomplished poet and essay writer, she is currently working on her first juvenile novel. Audrey would like to dedicate *The Day the Gypsies Came to Town* "to the memory of my parents who gave me my happy childhood."

Douglas Oudekerk was born in Glens Falls, New York. With a fine arts education from a variety of institutions, including State University College of New York (Oswego), the University of Minnesota, and the Minneapolis College of Art and Design, he has a wide background in illustration, commercial art, photography, technical drawing, and printmaking. Doug is currently a freelance illustrator, contributing his talents to numerous magazines, newspapers, and publications.

Rena C. Gropper, Professor of Applied Anthropology at Hunter College, New York, and the author of many works on Gypsies, including the book *Gypsies in the City*, deserves special thanks for her consultation on both the text and the illustrations.

Published by Raintree Publishers Inc., 330 E. Kilbourn Avenue, Milwaukee, Wisconsin 53202

Art Direction: Jenny Franz

Printed in the United States of America.   2 3 4 5 6 7 8 9 0 87 86 85 84

Library of Congress Cataloging in Publication Data
Masterson, Audrey Nelson.   The day the Gypsies came to town.   "A Carnival Press book."
Summary: Abby befriends a young Gypsy boy passing through her Midwestern town in the 1920's.
[1. Gypsies—Fiction.   2. Friendship—Fiction]   I. Oudekerk, Douglas, ill.   II. Title.
PZ7.M42395Day   1983   [E]   83-7319   ISBN 0-940742-22-5